I0761320

AESOP'S FABLES

FEATURING ILLUSTRATIONS BY ERIC CARLE

PETER PAUPER PRESS, INC.
Rye Brook, New York

PETER PAUPER PRESS
Fine Books and Gifts Since 1928

Our Company

In 1928, at the age of twenty-two, Peter Beilenson began printing books on a small press in the basement of his parents' home in Larchmont, New York. Peter—and later, his wife, Edna—sought to create fine books that sold at "prices even a pauper could afford."

Today, still family owned and operated, Peter Pauper Press continues to honor our founders' legacy—and our customers' expectations—of beauty, quality, and value.

Designed by Margaret Rubiano

3 International Drive
Rye Brook, NY 10573 USA

Published in the UK and Europe by Peter Pauper Press, Inc.
c/o White Pebble International
Units 2-3, Spring Business Park
Stanbridge Road
Havant, Hampshire PO9 2GJ, UK

Library of Congress Control Number: 2023942014

ISBN 978-1-4413-4258-4
Printed in China

7 6 5 4 3 2 1

www.peterpauper.com

CONTENTS

THE GOOSE AND THE GOLDEN EGG

THERE WAS ONCE a Countryman who possessed the most wonderful Goose you can imagine, for every day when he visited the nest, the Goose had laid a beautiful, glittering, golden egg.

The Countryman took the eggs to market and soon began to get rich. But it was not long before he grew impatient with the Goose because she gave him only a single golden egg a day. He was not getting rich fast enough.

Then one day, after he had finished counting his money, the idea came to him that he could get all the golden eggs at once by killing the Goose and cutting it open. But when the deed was done, not a single golden egg did he find, and his precious Goose was dead.

Those who have plenty want more and so lose all they have.

THE WOLF AND THE KID

THERE WAS ONCE a little Kid who liked to think he was all grown up and could take care of himself. So one evening when the flock started home from the pasture and his mother called, the Kid paid no heed and kept right on nibbling the tender grass. A little later when he lifted his head, the flock was gone.

He was all alone. The sun was sinking. Long shadows came creeping over the ground. A chill wind came creeping with them through the grass. The Kid shivered and began looking for his flock, running wildly across the field. But soon, near a clump of trees, he saw the terrible Wolf!

The Kid knew there was little hope for him.

"Please, Mr. Wolf," he said, "I know you are going to eat me. But first please pipe me a tune, for I want to dance for as long as I can."

The Wolf liked the idea of a little music before eating, so he struck up a tune.

Meanwhile, the flock was moving slowly homeward. In the still evening air, the Wolf's piping carried far. The Shepherd Dogs recognized the Wolf's song, and in a moment they were racing back to the pasture. As the Wolf ran, with the Dogs at his heels, he called himself a fool for making music when he should have just made dinner.

Do not let anything turn you from your purpose.

THE TORTOISE AND THE DUCKS

ONCE THERE WAS a Tortoise who wanted to see the world, and when he saw the birds fly about and the Hare and the Chipmunk run nimbly by, he felt very sad and discontented. He wanted to travel, too, but he carried his house on his back and could not go far or fast.

One day he met a pair of Ducks and told them all his troubles.

"We can help you to see the world," said the Ducks. "Take hold of this stick with your teeth and we will carry you to where you can see the whole countryside. But keep quiet or you will be sorry."

The Tortoise was very glad indeed. He seized the stick, the two Ducks took hold of it, and away they sailed up toward the clouds.

Just then a Crow flew by. He was very much astonished at the strange sight and cried: "This must surely be the King of Tortoises!"

"Why certainly—" began the Tortoise.

But as he opened his mouth to speak he lost his hold on the stick, and down he fell to the ground, where he was dashed to pieces on a rock.

Foolish curiosity and vanity often lead to misfortune.

THE YOUNG CRAB AND HIS MOTHER

"Why in the world do you walk sideways like that?" said a Mother Crab to her son. "You should always walk straight forward with your toes turned out."

"Show me how to walk, mother dear," answered the little Crab obediently, "I want to learn."

So the old Crab tried to walk straight forward. But she could walk sideways only, like her son. And when she tried to turn her toes out she tripped and fell on her nose.

Do not tell others how to act unless you can set a good example.

THE GNAT AND THE BULL

A Gnat flew over the meadow with much buzzing for so small a creature and settled on the tip of one of the horns of a Bull. After he had rested a short time, he made ready to fly away. But before he left he begged the Bull's pardon for having used his horn for a resting place.

"You must be very glad to have me go now," he said.

"It's all the same to me," replied the Bull. "I did not even know you were there."

We are often of greater importance in our own eyes than in the eyes of our neighbor.

The smaller the mind the greater the conceit.

THE FROGS AND THE OX

An Ox came down to a reedy pool to drink. As he splashed heavily into the water, he crushed a young Frog into the mud. The old Frog soon missed the little one and asked his siblings what had become of him.

"A great big monster," said one of them, "stepped on little brother with one of his huge feet!"

"Big, was he!" said the old Frog, puffing herself up. "Was he as big as this?"

"Oh, much bigger!" they cried.

The old Frog puffed up still more. But the little Frogs declared the monster was much, much bigger and the old Frog kept puffing herself up until, all at once, she burst.

Do not attempt the impossible.

THE CROW AND THE PITCHER

In a spell of dry weather, when the Birds could find very little to drink, a thirsty Crow found a pitcher with a little water in it. But the pitcher was high and had a narrow neck, and no matter how he tried, the Crow could not reach the water. The poor thing felt as if he must die of thirst.

Then an idea came to him. Picking up some small pebbles, he dropped them into the pitcher one by one. With each pebble the water rose a little higher until at last it was near enough so he could drink.

In a pinch a good use of our wits may help us out.

THE HARE AND THE TORTOISE

A Hare was making fun of the Tortoise one day for being so slow.

"Do you ever get anywhere?" he asked with a mocking laugh.

"Yes," replied the Tortoise, "and I get there sooner than you think. I'll run you a race and prove it."

The Hare was much amused at the idea of running a race with the Tortoise, but for the fun of the thing he agreed. So the Fox, who had consented to act as judge, marked the distance and started the runners off.

The Hare was soon far out of sight, and to make the Tortoise feel very deeply how ridiculous it was for him to try a race with a Hare, he lay down beside the course to take a nap until the Tortoise should catch up.

The Tortoise meanwhile kept going slowly but steadily, and, after a time, passed the place where the Hare was sleeping. But the Hare slept on very peacefully; and when at last he did wake up, the Tortoise was near the goal. The Hare now ran his fastest, but he could not overtake the Tortoise in time.

The race is not always to the swift.

THE DOG, THE ROOSTER, AND THE FOX

A Dog and a Rooster, who were the best of friends, wished very much to see the world. So they decided to leave the farmyard and travel along the road that led to the woods.

At nightfall the Rooster, looking for a place to perch, spied nearby a hollow tree to rest for the night. The Dog could creep inside and the Rooster would fly up on one of the branches. So said, so done, and both slept very comfortably.

At dawn, the Rooster awoke. Forgetting that he was no longer in the farmyard, he flapped his wings and crowed. But instead of awakening the farmer, he awakened a nearby Fox. Imagining a delicious breakfast, the Fox hurried to the tree where the Rooster sat, and said:

"A hearty welcome to our woods. I am sure we shall become the closest of friends."

"I feel highly flattered," replied the Rooster slyly. "If you will please go around to the door of my house at the foot of the tree, my porter will let you in."

The hungry Fox went around the tree as he was told, and in a moment was seized by the Dog.

Those who try to deceive may expect to be paid in their own coin.

BELLING THE CAT

The Mice once called a meeting to decide on a plan to free themselves of their enemy, the Cat. At least they wished to find some way of knowing when she was coming, so they might have time to run away.

Many plans were discussed, but none of them was thought good enough. At last a very young Mouse got up and said:

"I have a plan that seems very simple, but I know it will be successful. All we have to do is to hang a bell about the Cat's neck. When we hear the bell ringing we will know immediately that our enemy is coming."

All the Mice were much surprised that they had not thought of such a plan before. But in the midst of the rejoicing over their good fortune, an old Mouse arose and said:

"I will say that the plan of the young Mouse is very good. But let me ask one question: Who will bell the Cat?"

It is one thing to say that something should be done, but quite a different matter to do it.

THE LION AND THE MOUSE

A LION LAY asleep in the forest, his great head resting on his paws. A timid little Mouse came upon him unexpectedly, and in her fright and haste to get away, ran across the Lion's nose. Roused from his nap, the Lion laid his huge paw angrily on the tiny creature to kill her.

"Spare me!" begged the poor Mouse. "Please let me go and someday I will surely repay you."

The Lion was much amused to think that a Mouse could ever help him. But he was generous and finally let the Mouse go.

Some days later, while stalking his prey in the forest, the Lion was caught in the toils of a hunter's net. Unable to free himself, he filled the forest with his angry roaring. The Mouse knew the voice and quickly found the Lion struggling in the net. Running to one of the great ropes that bound him, she gnawed it until it parted, and soon the Lion was free.

"You laughed when I said I would repay you," said the Mouse. "Now you see that even a Mouse can help a Lion."

A kindness is never wasted.

THE TOWN MOUSE AND THE COUNTRY MOUSE

A Town Mouse once visited a relative who lived in the country. For lunch the Country Mouse served wheat stalks, roots, acorns, and cold water for drink. The Town Mouse had very little, only eating the simple food to be polite.

After the meal, the Town Mouse talked about her life in the city. The two then went to bed in a cozy nest in the hedgerow. That night, the Country Mouse dreamed of all the delights of city life. So the next day when the Town Mouse asked the Country Mouse to go home with her to the city, she gladly said yes.

When they reached the mansion in which the Town Mouse lived, they found pastries and delicious cheeses on the table. But as they were about to eat, they heard a Cat scratch at the door. The Mice scurried away and hid for a long time. When at last they ventured back to the feast, they saw servants clearing the table, followed by the House Dog.

The Country Mouse stayed only long enough to pick up her things.

"You may have luxuries," she said, "but I prefer my simple life in the country with the peace that goes with it."

Poverty with security is better than plenty
in the midst of fear and uncertainty.

THE SHEPHERD BOY AND THE WOLF

A SHEPHERD BOY tended Sheep near a dark forest not far from the village. As the days wore on, he found his work to be very dull. One day as he sat watching the Sheep and the quiet forest, he thought of a plan to amuse himself.

He knew that if he called for help should a Wolf attack the flock, the Villagers would drive it away. So although he had not seen anything that even looked like a Wolf, he ran toward the village shouting at the top of his voice, "Wolf! Wolf!"

The Villagers dropped their work and ran to the pasture. But when they got there they found the Boy doubled up with laughter.

A few days later the Shepherd Boy again shouted, "Wolf! Wolf!" Again the Villagers ran to help him, only to be laughed at once more.

Then one evening not long after, a Wolf really did spring from the underbrush and fall upon the Sheep.

In terror the Boy ran toward the village shouting "Wolf! Wolf!" But though the Villagers heard the cry, they did not run to help him. "He cannot fool us again," they said.

The Wolf killed a great many of the Boy's sheep before slipping away into the forest.

Liars are not believed even when they speak the truth.

THE ROSE AND THE BUTTERFLY

A BUTTERFLY ONCE fell in love with a beautiful Rose. The Rose was not indifferent, for the Butterfly's wings were powdered in a charming pattern of gold and silver. And so, when he fluttered near and told how he loved her, she blushed rosily and said yes. After many whispered vows of constancy, the Butterfly took a tender leave of his sweetheart.

But alas! It was a long time before he came back to see her.

"Is this your constancy?" she exclaimed tearfully. "It is ages since you went away, and all the time, you have been carrying on with all sorts of flowers. I saw you kiss Miss Geranium, and you fluttered around Miss Mignonette until Honeybee chased you away. I wish he had stung you!"

"Constancy!" laughed the Butterfly. "I had no sooner left you than I saw Zephyr kissing you. You carried on scandalously with Mr. Bumble Bee and you made eyes at every single Bug you could see. You can't expect any constancy from me!"

Do not expect constancy in others if you have none yourself.

THE SHEEP AND THE PIG

One day a Shepherd discovered a fat Pig in the meadow where his Sheep were pastured. He very quickly captured the porker, which squealed at the top of its voice the moment the Shepherd laid his hands on it. You would have thought, to hear the loud squealing, that the Pig was being cruelly hurt. But in spite of its squeals and struggles to escape, the Shepherd tucked his prize under his arm and started off to the butcher's in the marketplace.

The Sheep in the pasture were much astonished and amused at the Pig's behavior, and followed the Shepherd and his charge to the pasture gate.

"What makes you squeal like that?" asked one of the Sheep. "The Shepherd often catches and carries off one of us. But we should feel very much ashamed to make such a terrible fuss about it like you do."

"That is all very well," replied the Pig, with a squeal and a frantic kick. "When he catches you he is only after your wool. But he wants my bacon! *Gree-ee-ee!*"

It is easy to be brave when there is no danger.

THE EAGLE AND THE KITE

AN EAGLE SAT high in the branches of a great Oak. She seemed very sad and drooping for an Eagle. A Kite saw her.

"Why do you look so sorrowful?" asked the Kite.

"I want to get married," replied the Eagle, "and I can't find a mate who can provide for me as I should like."

"Take me," said the Kite; "I am very strong, stronger even than you!"

"Do you really think you can provide for me?" asked the Eagle eagerly.

"Why, of course," replied the Kite. "That would be a very simple matter. I am so strong I can carry away an Ostrich in my talons as if it were a feather!"

The Eagle was thrilled, and accepted the Kite immediately. But after the wedding, when the Kite flew away to find something to eat for his bride, all he returned with was a tiny Mouse.

"Is that the Ostrich you talked about?" said the Eagle in disgust.

"To win you, I would have said and promised anything," replied the Kite.

Everything is fair in love.

THE OAK AND THE REEDS

A GIANT OAK stood near a brook in which grew some slender Reeds. When the wind blew, the great Oak stood proudly upright with its hundred arms uplifted to the sky. But the Reeds bowed low in the wind and sang a sad and mournful song.

"You have reason to complain," said the Oak. "The slightest breeze that ruffles the surface of the water makes you bow your heads, while I, the mighty Oak, stand upright and firm before the howling tempest."

"Do not worry about us," replied the Reeds. "The winds do not harm us. We bow before them and so we do not break. You, in all your pride and strength, have so far resisted their blows. But the end is coming."

As the Reeds spoke a great hurricane rushed out of the north. The Oak stood proudly and fought against the storm, while the yielding Reeds bowed low. The wind redoubled in fury, and all at once the great tree fell, torn up by the roots, and lay among the pitying Reeds.

Better to yield when it is folly to resist, than to resist stubbornly and be destroyed.

THE TRAVELERS AND THE PURSE

Two men were traveling in company along the road when one of them picked up a well-filled purse.

"How lucky I am!" he said. "I have found a purse. Judging by its weight it must be full of gold."

"Do not say 'I have found a purse,'" said his companion. "Say rather 'we have found a purse' and 'how lucky we are.' Travelers ought to share alike the fortunes or misfortunes of the road."

"No, no," replied the other angrily. "I found it and I am going to keep it."

Just then they heard a shout of "Stop, thief!" and looking around, saw a mob of people armed with clubs coming down the road.

The man who had found the purse fell into a panic.

"We are lost if they find the purse on us," he cried.

"No, no," replied the other, "You would not say 'we' before, so now stick to your 'I.' Say 'I am lost.'"

We cannot expect anyone to share our misfortunes unless we are willing to share our good fortune also.

MERCURY AND THE WOODSMAN

Once, as a poor Woodsman was cutting down a tree, his axe slipped out of his hands into a nearby pool. He was in despair—he could not afford a day of lost work, nor could he afford a new axe. As he stood weeping, the god Mercury suddenly appeared. The Woodsman told Mercury his troubles, and straightway the kind Mercury dived into the pool and reappeared with a sparkling golden axe.

"Is this your axe?" asked Mercury.

"No," answered the Woodsman.

Mercury then presented a silver axe, but the Woodsman declared again that it was not his.

Finally, Mercury brought up the lost axe, and was so pleased with the Woodsman's honesty that he rewarded him with the gold and silver axes in addition to his own.

When the other Woodsmen heard this story, they hatched a plan for their own fortune. They hurried out into the woods and hid their axes. Then they wept and called on Mercury to help them.

And indeed, Mercury did appear. To each one he showed a golden axe, and each one claimed it to be the one he had lost. Mercury, furious with this deceit, sent them home. And when the Woodsmen returned next day to look for their own axes, they were nowhere to be found.

Honesty is the best policy.

THE FROGS WHO WISHED FOR A KING

The Frogs were tired of governing themselves. They had so much freedom that it had spoiled them, and they did nothing but sit around croaking in a bored manner and wishing for a government that could entertain them. So they sent a petition to Jupiter asking for a king.

To keep them quiet and make them think they had a king, Jupiter threw down a huge log, which fell into the water with a great splash. The Frogs hid among the reeds, thinking the new king to be some fearful giant. But they soon discovered how tame and peaceful King Log was. In a short time, the younger Frogs were using him for a diving platform, while the older Frogs made him a meeting place, where they complained loudly to Jupiter about the government.

To teach the Frogs a lesson the ruler of the gods now sent a Crane to be king of Frogland. The Crane proved to be a very different sort of king from old King Log. He gobbled up the poor Frogs right and left. In mournful croaks they begged Jupiter to take away the cruel tyrant before they should all be destroyed.

"How now!" cried Jupiter. "Are you not yet content? You have what you asked for and so you have only yourselves to blame."

Be sure you can better your condition before you seek to change it.

THE WOLF AND HIS SHADOW

A Wolf left his lair one evening in fine spirits and an excellent appetite. As he ran, the setting sun cast his shadow far out on the ground, and it looked as if the Wolf were a hundred times bigger than he really was.

"Why," exclaimed the Wolf proudly, "see how big I am! Fancy me running away from a puny Lion! I'll show him who is fit to be king, he or I."

Just then an immense shadow blotted him out entirely, and the next instant a Lion struck him down with a single blow.

Do not let your fancy make you forget realities.

THE FARMER AND THE STORK

A trusting Stork was once asked by a party of Cranes to visit a field that had been newly planted. But the party ended dismally with all the birds entangled in the meshes of the Farmer's net.

The Stork begged the Farmer to spare him.

"Please let me go," he pleaded. "I am an honest Stork. I did not know the Cranes were going to steal."

"You may be a very good bird," answered the Farmer, "but I caught you with the thieving Cranes and you will have to share the same punishment with them."

You are judged by the company you keep.

THE EAGLE AND THE BEETLE

A Beetle once begged an Eagle to spare a Hare which had run to her for protection. But the Eagle pounced upon her prey, the sweep of her great wings tumbling the Beetle a dozen feet away. Furious at the disrespect shown her, the Beetle flew to the Eagle's nest and rolled out the eggs. Not one did she spare. The Eagle's grief and anger knew no bounds, but who had done the cruel deed she did not know.

Next year the Eagle built her nest far up on a mountain crag; but the Beetle found it and again destroyed the eggs. In despair the Eagle now implored great Jupiter to let her place her eggs in his lap. There none would dare harm them. But the Beetle buzzed about Jupiter's head, and made him rise to drive her away; and the eggs rolled from his lap.

Now the Beetle told the reason for her action, and Jupiter had to acknowledge the justice of her cause. And they say that ever after, the Eagle's eggs lie in the nest in the spring season, while the Beetle still sleeps in the ground. For so Jupiter commanded.

Even the weakest may find means to avenge a wrong.

THE ANTS AND THE GRASSHOPPER

ONE BRIGHT DAY in late autumn a family of Ants were bustling about in the warm sunshine, drying out the grain they had stored up during the summer, when a starving Grasshopper, his fiddle under his arm, came up and humbly begged for a bite to eat.

"What!" cried the Ants in surprise, "haven't you stored anything away for the winter? What in the world were you doing all last summer?"

"I didn't have time to store up any food," whined the Grasshopper; "I was so busy making music that before I knew it the summer was gone."

The Ants shrugged their shoulders in disgust.

"Making music, were you?" they cried. "Very well; now dance!" And they turned their backs on the Grasshopper and went on with their work.

There's a time for work and a time for play.

THE LION AND THE GNAT

"Away with you, vile insect!" said a Lion angrily to a Gnat that was buzzing around his head. But the Gnat was not in the least disturbed.

"Do you think," he said spitefully to the Lion, "that I am afraid of you because they call you king?"

The next instant he flew at the Lion and stung him sharply on the nose. Mad with rage, the Lion struck fiercely at the Gnat, but only succeeded in tearing himself with his claws. Again and again the Gnat stung the Lion, who now was roaring terribly. At last, worn out with rage and covered with wounds that his own teeth and claws had made, the Lion gave up the fight.

The Gnat buzzed away to tell the whole world about his victory, but instead he flew straight into a Spider's web. And there, he who had defeated the King of Beasts came to a miserable end, the prey of a little Spider.

The least of our enemies is often the most to be feared.

Pride over a success should not throw us off our guard.

THE MONKEY AND THE CAMEL

AT A GREAT celebration in honor of King Lion, the Monkey was asked to dance for the company. His dancing was very clever indeed, and the animals were all highly pleased with his grace and lightness.

The praise that was showered on the Monkey made the Camel envious. He was very sure that he could dance quite as well as the Monkey, if not better, so he pushed his way into the crowd that was gathered around the Monkey, and rising on his hind legs, began to dance. But the big hulking Camel made himself very ridiculous as he kicked out his knotty legs and twisted his long clumsy neck. Besides, the animals found it hard to keep their toes from under his heavy hooves.

At last, when one of his huge feet came within an inch of King Lion's nose, the animals were so disgusted that they set upon the Camel in a rage and drove him out into the desert.

Shortly afterward, refreshments, consisting mostly of the Camel's hump and ribs, were served to the company.

Do not try to ape your betters.

THE WILD BOAR AND THE FOX

A WILD BOAR was sharpening his tusks busily against the stump of a tree, when a Fox happened by. The Fox was always looking for a chance to make fun of his neighbors, so he made a great show of looking about, as if afraid of some enemy. But the Boar kept right on with his work.

"Why are you doing that?" asked the Fox at last with a grin. "There isn't any danger that I can see."

"True enough," replied the Boar, "but when danger does come there will not be time for such work as this, so I must ready my weapons now."

Preparedness for war is the best guarantee of peace.

THE GOATHERD AND THE WILD GOATS

ONE COLD STORMY day a Goatherd drove his Goats for shelter into a cave, where he saw a number of Wild Goats. He wanted to make the Wild Goats part of his flock; so he fed them well. But to his own flock, he gave only just enough food to keep them alive. When the weather cleared, the Wild Goats scampered off to the hills.

"Is that the thanks I get for feeding you and treating you so well?" complained the Shepherd.

"We simply know how you would treat us later on," said a Wild Goat, "if some strangers should come as we did."

It is unwise to treat old friends badly for the sake of new ones.

THE FOX AND THE GRAPES

A Fox one day spied a beautiful bunch of ripe grapes hanging from a vine trained along the branches of a tree. The grapes seemed ready to burst with juice, and the Fox's mouth watered as he gazed longingly at them.

The bunch hung from a high branch, and the Fox had to jump for it. The first time he jumped he missed it by a long way. So he walked off a short distance and took a running leap at it, only to fall short once more. Again and again he tried, but in vain.

Now he sat down and looked at the grapes in disgust.

"What a fool I am," he said. "Here I am wearing myself out to get a bunch of sour grapes that are not worth gaping for."

And off he walked very, very scornfully.

There are many who pretend to despise and belittle that which is beyond their reach.

THE LION, THE BEAR, AND THE FOX

JUST AS A great Bear rushed to seize a stray Kid, a Lion leaped from another direction upon the same prey. The two fought furiously for the prize until, deeply wounded, they sank down, unable to continue the battle.

Just then a Fox dashed up, and seizing the Kid, made off with it as fast as he could go, while the Lion and the Bear looked on in helpless rage.

"How much better it would have been," they said, "to have shared in a friendly spirit."

Those who have all the toil do not always get the profit.

THE WOLF AND THE LION

A WOLF HAD stolen a Lamb and was carrying it off to his lair to eat. But his plans were changed when a Lion, without making any excuses, took the Lamb away from him.

The Wolf made off to a safe distance, and then said in a much injured tone:

"You have no right to take my property like that!"

The Lion looked back, but as the Wolf was too far away to be taught a lesson without too much inconvenience, he said:

"Your property? Did you buy it, or did the Shepherd make you a gift of it? Pray tell me, how did you get it?"

What is evil won is evil lost.

THE LION AND THE DONKEY

A Lion and a Donkey agreed to go hunting together. In their search for game the hunters saw a number of Wild Goats run into a cave, and laid plans to catch them. The Donkey was to go into the cave and drive the Goats out, while the Lion would stand at the entrance to strike them down.

The plan worked beautifully. The Donkey made such a frightful sight in the cave, kicking and braying with all his might, that the Goats came running out in a panic of fear, only to fall victim to the Lion.

The Donkey came proudly out of the cave.

"Did you see how I made them run?" he said.

"Yes, indeed," answered the Lion, "and if I had not known you and your kind I should certainly have run, too."

The loud-mouthed boaster does not impress nor frighten those who know him.

THE MICE AND THE WEASELS

The Weasels and the Mice were always up in arms against each other. In every battle the Weasels carried off the victory, as well as a large number of the Mice, which they ate for dinner next day. In despair the Mice called a council, and there it was decided that the Mouse army was always beaten because it had no leaders. So a large number of generals and commanders were appointed from among the most eminent Mice.

To distinguish themselves from the soldiers in the ranks, the new leaders proudly bound on their heads lofty crests and ornaments of feathers or straw. Then after long preparation of the Mouse army in all the arts of war, they sent a challenge to the Weasels.

The Weasels accepted the challenge with eagerness, for they were always ready for a fight when a meal was in sight. They immediately attacked the Mouse army in large numbers. Soon the Mouse line gave way before the attack and the whole army fled for cover. The privates easily slipped into their holes, but the Mouse leaders could not squeeze through the narrow openings because of their extravagant dress. Not one of them escaped the teeth of the hungry Weasels.

Greatness has its penalties.

THE WOLF AND THE DONKEY

A DONKEY WAS feeding in a pasture near a wood when he saw a Wolf lurking in the shadows along the hedge. He easily guessed what the Wolf had in mind, and thought of a plan to save himself. So he pretended he was lame, and began to hobble painfully.

When the Wolf came up, he asked the Donkey what had made him lame, and the Donkey replied that he had stepped on a sharp thorn.

"Please pull it out," he pleaded, groaning as if in pain. "If you do not, the thorn might stick in your throat when you eat me."

The Wolf saw the wisdom of the advice, for he wanted to enjoy his meal without any danger of choking. So the Donkey lifted up his foot and the Wolf began to search very closely and carefully for the thorn.

Just then the Donkey kicked out with all his might, tumbling the Wolf a dozen paces away. And while the Wolf was getting very slowly and painfully to his feet, the Donkey galloped away to safety.

"Serves me right," growled the Wolf as he crept into the bushes. "I'm a butcher by trade, not a doctor."

Stick to your trade.

THE HORSE AND THE STAG

THERE WAS ONCE a Horse who had a meadow all to himself until a Stag came along and decided that he wanted the pasture for his own use. After some quarreling, the Stag ousted the Horse from the meadow. Seeking revenge, the Horse went to the Hunter for assistance.

The Hunter agreed, but said: "If you desire to conquer the Stag, you must permit me to place this piece of iron between your jaws, so that I may guide you with these reins, and allow this saddle to be placed upon your back, so that I may keep steady upon you as we follow after the enemy."

The Horse agreed to the conditions, and the Hunter soon saddled and bridled him. Then with the aid of the Hunter the Horse soon overcame the Stag, and said to the Hunter: "Now, get off, and remove those things from my mouth and back."

"Not so fast, friend," said the Hunter. "I have now got you under bit and spur, and prefer to keep you as you are at present."

If you allow men to use you for your own purposes, they will use you for theirs.

THE MONKEY AND THE DOLPHIN

ONCE UPON A time a ship bound for Athens was wrecked off the coast close to Piraeus, Athens' port. Had it not been for the Dolphins, all would have perished. But the Dolphins took the shipwrecked people on their backs and swam with them to shore.

Sailors often brought their pet Monkeys with them whenever they went on a voyage. So when one of the Dolphins saw a Monkey struggling in the water, he thought it was a man, and made the Monkey climb up on his back.

The Monkey sat up, grave and dignified, on the Dolphin's back.

"Are you a citizen of Athens?" asked the Dolphin politely.

"Yes," answered the Monkey, proudly. "My family is one of the noblest in the city."

"Indeed," said the Dolphin. "Then of course you often visit Piraeus."

"Yes, yes," replied the Monkey. "Indeed, I do. I am with him constantly. Piraeus is my very best friend."

This answer surprised the Dolphin, and turning his head, he now saw what it was he was carrying. Without more ado, he dived and left the foolish Monkey to take care of himself, while he swam off in search of some human being to save.

One falsehood leads to another.

THE BEAR AND THE BEES

ONCE, A BEAR roaming the woods happened on a fallen tree in which a swarm of Bees had stored their honey. Hoping to take some for himself, he began to nose around the log very carefully. However, a stray Bee spotted him, and guessing what the Bear was after, stung him sharply before disappearing into the hollow log.

The Bear immediately lost his temper and sprang upon the log tooth and claw. But this only brought out the whole swarm. The poor Bear was forced to run, and could only save himself by diving into a pool of water.

It is wiser to bear a single injury in silence than to provoke a thousand by flying into a rage.

THE DOG IN THE MANGER

A DOG ASLEEP in a manger filled with hay, was awakened by the Cattle, which came in tired and hungry from working in the field. But when they tried to eat, the Dog snarled and snapped furiously.

The Cattle looked at the Dog in disgust. "How selfish he is!" said one. "He cannot eat the hay and yet he will not let us eat it who are so hungry for it!"

But the Dog would not quit until the farmer forced him out of the stable as punishment for his selfishness.

Do not grudge others what you cannot enjoy yourself.

THE STAG AND HIS REFLECTION

A STAG, DRINKING from a crystal spring, saw himself mirrored in the clear water. He greatly admired the graceful arch of his antlers, but he was very much ashamed of his spindling legs.

"How can it be," he sighed, "that I should be cursed with such legs when I have so magnificent a crown."

At that moment he scented a Panther and in an instant was bounding away through the forest. But as he ran his wide-spreading antlers caught in the branches of the trees, and soon the Panther overtook him. Then the Stag perceived that the legs of which he was so ashamed would have saved him had it not been for the useless ornaments on his head.

We often make much of the ornamental and despise the useful.

THE WOLF AND THE GOAT

A HUNGRY WOLF spied a Goat browsing at the top of a steep cliff where he could not possibly get at her.

"That is a very dangerous place for you," he called out, pretending to worry for the Goat's safety. "Please listen to me and come down! Here you can eat the finest, tenderest grass in the country."

The Goat looked over the edge of the cliff.

"How very anxious you are about me," she said, "and how generous you are with your grass! But I know you. It's your own appetite you are thinking of, not mine!"

An invitation prompted by selfishness is not to be accepted.

THE WOLF IN SHEEP'S CLOTHING

A CERTAIN WOLF could not get enough to eat because of the watchfulness of the Shepherds. But one night he found a sheepskin that had been cast aside and forgotten. The next day, dressed in the skin, the Wolf strolled into the pasture with the Sheep. Soon enough, he had his next meal.

That evening, the Wolf entered the fold with the flock. But it happened that the Shepherd took a fancy for mutton broth that very night, and, picking up a knife, went to the fold. There the first he laid hands on and killed was the Wolf.

The evildoer often comes to harm through his own deceit.

THE CAT, THE ROOSTER, AND THE YOUNG MOUSE

A VERY YOUNG Mouse, who had never seen anything of the world, almost came to grief the very first time he ventured out. And this is the story he told his mother about his adventures.

"I was strolling along when I saw two strange creatures. One of them had a very kind look, but the other was a fearful monster. On his head and neck hung pieces of raw red meat. He walked about restlessly, tearing up the ground with his toes. When he saw me, he opened his pointed mouth as if to swallow me whole and then let out a piercing roar.

"If it had not been for that terrible monster," the Mouse went on, "I should have met the gentle creature. He had velvety fur and shining eyes. He waved his fine long tail and smiled at me. I was about to speak with him, but when the monster let out a screaming yell, I left before saying hello."

"My son," said the Mother Mouse, "that gentle creature you saw was none other than the Cat. The other was nothing but a bird who wouldn't harm you in the least. As for the Cat, he eats us. So be thankful that you escaped with your life, and, as long as you live, never judge people by their looks."

Do not trust alone outward appearances.

THE FOX AND THE ROOSTER

A Fox was caught in a trap one fine morning, because he had got too near the Farmer's henhouse. No doubt he was hungry, but that was not an excuse for stealing. A Rooster, rising early, discovered what had happened. He knew the Fox could not get at him, so he went a little closer to get a good look at his enemy.

The Fox saw a slender chance of escape.

"Dear friend," he said, "I was just on my way to visit a sick relative, when I stumbled into this string and got all tangled up. But please do not tell anybody about it. I dislike causing sorrow to anybody, and I am sure I can soon gnaw this string to pieces."

But the Rooster was not to be so easily fooled. He soon roused the whole hen yard, and when the Farmer came running out, that was the end of Mr. Fox.

The wicked deserve no aid.

THE SPENDTHRIFT AND THE SWALLOW

A young fellow, who was very popular among his companions as a good spender, quickly wasted his fortune trying to live up to his reputation. Then one fine day in early spring he found himself with not a penny left, and no property save the clothes he wore.

He was to meet some jolly friends that morning, and he was at his wits' end how to get enough money to keep up appearances. Just then a Swallow flew by, twittering merrily, and the young Man, thinking summer had come, hastened off to a clothes dealer, to whom he sold all the clothes he wore down to his very tunic.

A few days later a change in weather brought a severe frost; and the poor Swallow and that foolish young Man in his light tunic, with his arms and knees bare, could scarcely keep life in their shivering bodies.

One swallow does not make a summer.

THE CAT AND THE FOX

ONCE A CAT and a Fox were traveling together. As they went along, picking up provisions on the way—a stray mouse here, a fat chicken there—they began an argument to while away the time between bites. And, as usually happens when comrades argue, the talk began to get personal.

"You think you are extremely clever, don't you?" said the Fox. "Do you pretend to know more than I? Why, I know a whole sackful of tricks!"

"Well," retorted the Cat, "I admit I know one trick only, but that one, let me tell you, is worth a thousand of yours!"

Just then, close by, they heard a hunter's horn and the yelping of a pack of hounds. In an instant the Cat was up a tree, hiding among the leaves.

"This is my trick," he called to the Fox. "Now let me see what yours are worth."

But the Fox had so many plans for escape he could not decide which one to try first. He dodged here and there with the hounds at his heels. He doubled on his tracks, he ran at top speed, he entered a dozen burrows—but all in vain. The hounds caught him, and soon put an end to the boaster.

Common sense is always worth more than cunning.

THE ASTROLOGER

A MAN WHO lived a long time ago believed that he could read the future in the stars. He called himself an Astrologer, and spent his time at night gazing at the sky.

One evening he was walking along the open road outside the village. His eyes were fixed on the stars. He thought he saw there that the end of the world was at hand, when all at once, down he went into a hole filled to the brim with mud and water.

There he stood up to his ears, in the muddy water, and madly clawing at the slippery sides of the hole in his effort to climb out.

His cries for help soon brought the villagers running. As they pulled him out of the mud, one of them said:

"You pretend to read the future in the stars, and yet you fail to see what is at your feet! What use is it to read the stars, when you can't see what's right in front of you on Earth?"

Take care of the little things and the big things will take care of themselves.

THREE BULLS AND A LION

A LION HAD been watching three Bulls feeding in an open field. He had tried to attack them several times, but the Bulls helped each other to drive him off. The Lion began to lose hope of eating them, for he was no match for the three together.

Then one day the Bulls had a quarrel, and when the hungry Lion came to look at them and lick his chops as he was accustomed to do, he found them in separate corners of the field, as far away from one another as they could get.

It was now an easy matter for the Lion to attack them one at a time, and this he proceeded to do with relish.

In unity is strength.

THE TRAVELERS AND THE SEA

TWO TRAVELERS WERE walking along the seashore. Far out they saw something riding on the waves.

"Look," said one, "a great ship comes bearing treasures!"

The object they saw came ever nearer to shore.

"No," said the other, "that is not a treasure ship. That is some fisherman's skiff, with the day's catch."

Nearer came the object. The waves washed it to shore.

"It is a chest of gold lost from some wreck," they cried. Both Travelers rushed to the beach, but there they found nothing but a water-soaked log.

Do not let your hopes carry you away from reality.

THE FROG AND THE MOUSE

A YOUNG MOUSE in search of adventure was running along the bank of a pond where a Frog lived. When the Frog saw the Mouse, he croaked:

"Won't you pay me a visit? I can promise you a good time if you do."

The Mouse did not need much coaxing, for he was very anxious to see the world and everything in it. But though he could swim a little, he did not dare risk going into the pond without some help.

The Frog had a plan. He tied the Mouse's leg to his own with a tough reed. Then into the pond he jumped, dragging his foolish companion with him.

The Mouse soon had enough of it and wanted to return to shore; but the treacherous Frog had other plans. He pulled the Mouse down under the water and drowned him. But before he could untie the reed that bound him to the dead Mouse, a Hawk came sailing over the pond. Seeing the body of the Mouse floating on the water, the Hawk swooped down, seized the Mouse and carried it off, with the Frog dangling from its leg. Thus at one swoop he had caught both meat and fish for his dinner.

Those who seek to harm others often come to harm themselves through their own deceit.

THE OLD LION AND THE FOX

AN OLD LION, whose teeth and claws were so worn that it was not so easy for him to get food as in his younger days, pretended that he was sick. He took care to let all his neighbors know about it, and then lay down in his cave to wait for visitors. And when they came to offer him their sympathy, he ate them up one by one.

The Fox came too, but he was very cautious about it. Standing at a safe distance from the cave, he inquired politely after the Lion's health. The Lion replied that he was very ill indeed, and asked the Fox to step in for a moment. But Master Fox very wisely stayed outside, thanking the Lion very kindly for the invitation.

"I should be glad to do as you ask," he added, "but I have noticed that there are many footprints leading into your cave and none coming out. Pray tell me, how do your visitors find their way out again?"

Take warning from the misfortunes of others.

THE MISER

A MISER HAD buried his gold in a secret place in his garden. Every day he went to the spot, dug up the treasure and counted it piece by piece. He made so many trips that a Thief, who had been observing him, guessed what it was the Miser had hidden, and one night quietly dug up the treasure and made off with it.

When the Miser discovered his loss, he was overcome with grief and despair. He groaned and cried and tore his hair.

A passerby heard his cries and asked what had happened.

"My gold! Oh, my gold!" cried the Miser. "Someone has robbed me!"

"Your gold! There in that hole? Why did you not keep it in the house where you could easily get it when you had to buy things?"

"Buy!" screamed the Miser, angrily. "Why, I never once touched the gold. I couldn't think of spending any of it."

The stranger picked up a large stone and threw it into the hole.

"If that is the case," he said, "cover up that stone. It is worth just as much to you as the treasure you lost!"

A possession is worth no more than the use we make of it.

THE MILKMAID AND HER PAIL

A MILKMAID HAD been out to milk the cows and was returning from the field with the shining milk pail balanced nicely on her head. As she walked along, her pretty head was busy with plans for the days to come.

"This good, rich milk," she mused, "will give me plenty of cream to churn. The butter I make I will take to market, and with the money I get for it I will buy a lot of eggs for hatching. How nice it will be when they are all hatched and the yard is full of fine young chicks. Then when May Day comes I will sell them, and with the money I'll buy a lovely new dress to wear to the fair. All the young men will look at me. They will come and try to woo me—but I shall very quickly send them about their business!"

As she thought of how she would settle that matter, she tossed her head scornfully, and down fell the pail of milk to the ground. And all the milk flowed out, and with it vanished butter and eggs and chicks and the new dress and all the milkmaid's pride.

Do not count your chickens before they are hatched.

THE BAT AND THE WEASELS

A Bat blundered into the nest of a Weasel, who ran up to catch and eat him. The Bat begged for his life, but the Weasel would not listen.

"You are a Mouse," he said, "and I am a sworn enemy of Mice. Every Mouse I catch, I am going to eat!"

"But I am not a Mouse!" cried the Bat. "Look at my wings. Can Mice fly? Why, I am only a Bird! Please let me go!"

The Weasel had to admit that the Bat was not a Mouse, so he let him go. But a few days later, the foolish Bat went blindly into the nest of another Weasel. This Weasel happened to be a bitter enemy of Birds, and he soon had the Bat under his claws, ready to eat him.

"You are a Bird," he said, "and I am going to eat you!"

"What," cried the Bat, "I, a Bird! Why, all Birds have feathers! I am nothing but a Mouse. 'Down with all Cats,' is my motto!"

And so the Bat escaped with his life a second time.

Set your sails with the wind.

THE FOX AND THE HEDGEHOG

A FOX, SWIMMING across a river, was barely able to reach the bank, where he lay bruised and exhausted from his struggle with the swift current. Soon a swarm of blood-sucking flies settled on him; but he lay quietly, still too weak to run away from them.

A Hedgehog happened by. "Let me drive the flies away," he said kindly.

"No, no!" exclaimed the Fox. "Do not disturb them! They have taken all they can hold. If you drive them away, another greedy swarm will come and take the little blood I have left."

Better to bear a lesser evil than to risk a greater in removing it.

THE ANT AND THE DOVE

A DOVE SAW an Ant fall into a brook. The Ant struggled to reach the bank, and in pity, the Dove dropped a blade of straw close beside it. Clinging to the straw like a shipwrecked sailor to a broken spar, the Ant floated safely to shore.

Soon after, the Ant saw a man getting ready to kill the Dove with a stone. But just as he cast the stone, the Ant stung him in the heel, so that the pain made him miss his aim, and the startled Dove flew to safety in a distant wood.

One good turn deserves another.

THE ROOSTER AND THE FOX

One bright evening as the sun was sinking on a glorious world a wise old Rooster flew into a tree to roost. But just as he was about to put his head under his wing, he caught sight of Master Fox.

"Have you heard the wonderful news?" cried the Fox.

The Rooster eyed him cautiously. "What news?"

"Your family and mine and all other animals have agreed to forget their differences and live in peace and friendship from now on forever. Just think of it! Do come down, dear friend, and let us celebrate the joyful event."

"How grand!" said the Rooster. "I certainly am delighted at the news." But he spoke in an absent way, and stretching up on tiptoes, seemed to be looking at something afar off.

"What is it you see?" asked the Fox a little anxiously.

"Why, it looks to me like a couple of Dogs coming this way. They must have heard the good news and—"

But the Fox did not wait to hear more and began to run.

"Wait," cried the Rooster. "Why do you run? The Dogs are friends of yours now!"

"Yes," answered the Fox. "But they might not have heard the news. Besides, I have a very important errand that I had almost forgotten about."

The Rooster smiled as he buried his head in his feathers and went to sleep, for he had succeeded in outwitting a very crafty enemy.

The trickster is easily tricked.

TWO TRAVELERS AND A BEAR

Two Men were traveling in company through a forest, when, all at once, a huge Bear crashed out of the brush near them.

One of the Men, thinking of his own safety, climbed a tree.

The other, unable to fight the savage beast alone, threw himself on the ground and lay still, as if he were dead. He had heard that a Bear will not touch a dead body.

It must have been true, for the Bear snuffed at the Man's head awhile, and then, seeming to be satisfied that he was dead, walked away.

The Man in the tree climbed down.

"It looked just as if that Bear whispered in your ear," he said. "What did he tell you?"

"He said," answered the other, "that it was not at all wise to keep company with a fellow who would desert his friend in a moment of danger."

Misfortune is the test of true friendship.

THE FOX WITHOUT A TAIL

A Fox that had been caught in a trap succeeded at last in getting away, but he had to leave his beautiful bushy tail behind to escape. For a long time after, he kept away from the other Foxes, for he knew that they would all make fun of him. But it was hard for him to live alone, so at last he called a meeting, saying that he had something of great importance to tell them.

When they were all gathered together, the Fox Without a Tail got up and made a speech about those Foxes who had come to harm because of their tails.

One had been caught by hounds when his tail got stuck in a hedge. Another was slowed by the weight of his brush. Besides, men hunt Foxes to display their tails. With such proof of danger, said Master Fox, he would advise every Fox to cut his tail off.

When he had finished talking, an old Fox arose, and said:

"Master Fox, turn around, and you shall have your answer."

When the poor Fox Without a Tail turned around, there arose such a storm of laughter, that he saw how useless it was to try any longer to persuade the Foxes to part with their tails.

Do not listen to the advice of him who seeks to lower you to his own level.

THE ANIMALS AND THE PLAGUE

ONCE UPON A time a severe plague raged among the animals. Many died, and those who lived lost their appetites entirely.

At last, the Lion called a council. He began:

"I believe the gods have sent this plague upon us as a punishment for our sins. Therefore, the most guilty one of us must be offered in sacrifice. I will confess first. I admit that I have devoured many sheep, although they had done me no harm."

"That's no sin," replied the Fox. "You have done the sheep a great honor by eating them."

All the animals agreed. Then, though all the savage beasts recited the most wicked deeds, all were excused and made to appear innocent.

Then it was the Donkey's turn. "One day," he said, "I ate some grass from a farmer's field. I had no right to do it, I admit—"

A great uproar among the beasts interrupted him. Here was the culprit who had brought misfortune on all of them! What a horrible crime it was to eat grass that belonged to someone else!

Immediately they all fell upon him, sacrificing him to the gods then and there, and without the formality of an altar.

The weak are made to suffer for the misdeeds of the powerful.

THE MOTHER AND THE WOLF

EARLY ONE MORNING a hungry Wolf was prowling around a cottage at the edge of a village, when he heard a child crying in the house. Then he heard the Mother's voice say:

"Hush, child, hush! Stop your crying, or I will give you to the Wolf!"

Surprised but delighted at the prospect of so delicious a meal, the Wolf settled down under an open window, expecting every moment to have the child handed out to him. But though the little one continued to fret, the Wolf waited all day in vain. Then, toward nightfall, he heard the Mother's voice again as she sat down near the window to sing and rock her baby to sleep.

"There, child, there! The Wolf shall not get you. No, no! Daddy is watching and Daddy will kill him if he should come near!"

Just then the Father came within sight of the home, and the Wolf was barely able to save himself from the Dogs by a clever bit of running.

Do not believe everything you hear.

THE WOLF AND THE HOUSE DOG

THERE WAS ONCE a Wolf who got very little to eat because the Dogs of the village were so watchful. One night he happened to fall in with a fine fat House Dog who had wandered a little too far from home. The Wolf complimented him on his fine appearance.

"You can eat as well as I do," replied the Dog. "In the woods, you have to fight hard for every bite you get. Follow my example and you will get along beautifully."

"What must I do?" asked the Wolf.

"Hardly anything," answered the House Dog. "Chase thieves, bark at intruders, and please the people of the house. In return you will get all the food you desire, not to speak of kind words and caresses."

The Wolf was thrilled at the prospect. But just then he noticed that the hair on the Dog's neck was worn.

"What is that on your neck?"

"Nothing at all," replied the Dog.

"Please, tell me!"

"Perhaps you see the mark of my collar."

"A collar!" cried the Wolf. "Don't you go wherever you please?"

"Not always! But what's the difference?" replied the Dog.

"All the difference in the world!" And away ran the Wolf to the woods.

There is nothing worth so much as liberty.

THE CAT AND THE OLD RAT

THERE WAS ONCE a Cat who was so watchful, that no Mice dared to cross him. In fact, the Mice stayed so far away, that the Cat knew he'd need to be clever to catch one. So one day he climbed up on a shelf and hung from it, holding himself up by clinging to some ropes with one paw.

When the Mice saw him in that position, they stuck out their heads and sniffed about carefully. But as nothing stirred, all trooped joyfully out to celebrate the death of the Cat. Just then the Cat let go his hold, capturing four mice before they could escape.

Now the Mice kept more strictly at home than ever. But the Cat, still hungry, knew more tricks than one. Rolling himself in flour until he was covered completely, he lay down in the flour bin, disguising himself as a fresh loaf of bread.

Sure enough, the Mice soon began to come out. The Cat was nearly ready to swipe when an old Rat, who had had much experience with Cats and traps, called out to the Mice.

"Take care! That may be a heap of meal, but it looks to me very much like the Cat. Be wise and keep yourselves far away."

The wise do not let themselves be tricked a second time.

THE BEES AND WASPS, AND THE HORNET

A STORE OF honey had been found in a hollow tree, and the Wasps declared that it belonged to them. The Bees were just as sure that the treasure was theirs. The argument grew very pointed, and eventually they agreed to let a judge decide the matter. So they brought the case before the Hornet, justice of the peace in that part of the woods.

When the Judge called the case, witnesses declared that they had seen certain winged creatures in the neighborhood of the hollow tree, who hummed loudly, and whose bodies were striped, yellow and black, like Bees.

Counsel for the Wasps immediately insisted that this description fitted his clients exactly.

Both sides brought forth more witnesses. Eventually, a wise old Bee addressed the Court.

"Your Honor," he said, "I move that the Bees and the Wasps be both instructed to build a honeycomb. Then we shall soon see to whom the honey really belongs."

The Wasps protested loudly. Wise Judge Hornet quickly understood why they did so. They knew they could not build a honeycomb and fill it with honey.

"It is clear," said the Judge, "who made the comb and who could not have made it. The honey belongs to the Bees."

Ability proves itself by deeds.

THE PEACOCK AND THE CRANE

A PEACOCK, PUFFED up with vanity, met a Crane one day, and to impress him spread his gorgeous tail in the sun so that each feather glittered like a jewel.

"Look," he said. "What have you to compare with this? I am dressed in all the glory of the rainbow, while your feathers are gray as dust!"

The Crane spread his broad wings and flew up toward the sun.

"Follow me if you can," he said. But the Peacock stood where he was among the birds of the barnyard, while the Crane soared in freedom far up into the blue sky.

The useful is of much more importance and value than the ornamental.

THE MAN AND THE SATYR

A LONG TIME ago a Man met a Satyr in the forest and succeeded in making friends with him. The two soon became the best of comrades, living together in the Man's hut. But one cold winter evening, as they were walking homeward, the Satyr saw the Man blow on his fingers.

"Why do you do that?" asked the Satyr.

"To warm my hands," the Man replied.

When they reached home the Man prepared two bowls of porridge. These he placed steaming hot on the table, and the comrades sat down very cheerfully to enjoy the meal. But much to the Satyr's surprise, the Man began to blow into his bowl of porridge.

"Why do you do that?" he asked.

"To cool my porridge," replied the Man.

The Satyr sprang hurriedly to his feet and made for the door.

"Goodbye," he said, "I've seen enough. A fellow that blows hot and cold in the same breath cannot be friends with me!"

The man who talks for both sides is not
to be trusted by either.

THE MILLER, HIS SON, AND THE DONKEY

One day, an old Miller and his Son traveled to market with a Donkey which they hoped to sell. As they walked along the highway some travelers began to laugh.

"How foolish!" cried one. "Why not ride the beast?"

The Miller did not like to be laughed at, so he told his Son to climb up and ride. Farther along the road, three merchants passed by.

"Young man!" they cried. "Show some respect, and let your father ride."

Though the Miller was not tired, he decided to climb up as well, just to please the Merchants. They had no sooner started out again when they heard another cry.

"How awful!" said one. "They look more able to carry the poor creature, than he to carry them."

The Miller and his Son quickly scrambled down, and a short time later, the marketplace was thrown into an uproar as the two came along carrying the Donkey slung from a pole. A great crowd of people gathered.

The laughter agitated the Donkey, who began to kick and bray. Then, just as they were crossing a bridge, the ropes that held him gave way, and the Donkey tumbled into the river.

The poor Miller now set out sadly for home. By trying to please everybody, he had pleased nobody, and lost his Donkey besides.

If you try to please all, you please none.

THE HORSE AND THE DONKEY

A Traveler with a Donkey and a Horse, who carried merchandise from town to town, was in the habit of letting the Donkey carry all the load.

One hot day, the Donkey was feeling very weak and sick, so she begged the Horse to carry some of the burden. "If I have to carry all of it today," she said, "I am going to collapse for good. But if you will take part of it, I will soon get well again and be able to carry it all."

But the Horse was proud and stubborn, and said he didn't want to be bothered with the complaining of a Donkey. The Donkey jogged on in silence; but soon, with the great heat and the heavy load, she fell down and died.

At this, the Traveler fastened the whole load on the Horse, and made him carry the dead Donkey besides, as far as the next tannery.

An unwilling partner is his own undoing.

THE WOLF, THE KID, AND THE GOAT

Mother Goat was going to market one morning to get provisions for her household, which consisted of but one little Kid and herself.

"Take good care of the house, my son," she said to the Kid, as she carefully latched the door. "Do not let anyone in, unless he gives you this password: 'Down with the Wolf!'"

Strangely enough, a Wolf was lurking near and heard what the Goat had said. So, as soon as Mother Goat was out of sight, up he trotted to the door and knocked.

"Down with the Wolf!" said the Wolf softly.

It was the right password, but when the Kid peeped through a crack in the door and saw the shadowy figure outside, he did not feel at all easy.

"Show me a white paw," he said, "or I won't let you inside."

A white paw, of course, is a feature few Wolves can show, and so Master Wolf had to go away as hungry as he had come.

"You can never be too sure," said the Kid when he saw the Wolf, downhearted and stomach growling, making off to the woods.

Two sureties are better than one.

THE ROOSTER AND THE JEWEL

A ROOSTER WAS busily scratching and scraping about to find something to eat for himself and his family, when he happened to turn up a precious jewel that had been lost by its owner.

"Aha!" said the Rooster. "No doubt you are very costly and he who lost you would give a great deal to find you. But as for me, I would choose a single grain of barleycorn before all the jewels in the world."

Precious things are without value to those who cannot prize them.

THE MULE

A MULE HAD had a long rest and much good feeding. He was feeling very vigorous indeed, and pranced around loftily, holding his head high.

"My father certainly was a full-blooded racer," he said. "I can feel that distinctly."

Next day he was put into harness again and that evening he was very downhearted indeed.

"I was mistaken," he said. "My father was a Donkey after all."

Be sure of your pedigree before you boast of it.

THE FOX AND THE CROW

One morning as the Fox was searching the woods for a bite to eat, he saw a Crow overhead, holding a bit of cheese in her beak.

"No need to search any farther," thought sly Master Fox. "Here is my breakfast."

Up he trotted to the foot of the tree in which the Crow was sitting, and looking up, he cried, "Good morning, beautiful creature!"

The Crow, her head cocked on one side, watched the Fox suspiciously, and kept her beak tightly closed on the cheese.

"What a charming creature she is!" said the Fox. "How her feathers shine! What splendid wings! Such a Bird should have a very lovely voice, since everything else about her is so perfect. Could she sing just one song, I know I should hail her Queen of Birds."

Listening to these flattering words, the Crow forgot all her suspicion. But when she opened her mouth to caw, her cheese fell straight into the Fox's open mouth.

"Thank you," said Master Fox sweetly, as he walked off. "You have a lovely voice sure enough. But where are your wits?"

The flatterer lives at the expense of those who will listen to him.

THE LEAP AT RHODES

A CERTAIN TRAVELER who visited foreign lands could talk of little when he returned to his home except the wonderful adventures he had met with and the great deeds he had done abroad.

One of the feats he told about was a leap he had made in a city called Rhodes. That leap was so great, he said, that no other man could leap anywhere near the distance. A great many persons in Rhodes had seen him do it and would prove that what he told was true.

"No need of witnesses," said one. "Suppose this city is Rhodes. Now show us how far you can jump."

Deeds count, not boasting words.

THE FISHERMAN AND THE LITTLE FISH

A POOR FISHERMAN had bad luck one day and caught nothing but a very small fry. He was about to put it in his basket when the little Fish said:

"Please spare me, Mr. Fisherman! I am so small it is not worthwhile to carry me home. When I am bigger, I shall make you a much better meal."

But the Fisherman quickly put the Fish into his basket.

"It would be foolish," he said, "to throw you back. You may be small, but you are better than nothing."

A small gain is worth more than a large promise.

THE LION, THE DONKEY, AND THE FOX

A Lion, a Donkey, and a Fox were hunting in company, and caught a large quantity of game. The Donkey was asked to divide the spoil. This he did very fairly, giving each an equal share.

The Fox was well satisfied, but the Lion flew into a great rage over it, and with one stroke of his huge paw, he added the Donkey to the pile of slain.

Then he turned to the Fox.

"You divide it," he roared angrily.

The Fox wasted no time in talking. He quickly piled all the game into one great heap. From this he took a very small portion for himself, such undesirable bits as the horns and hooves of a mountain goat, and the end of an ox tail.

The Lion now recovered his good humor entirely.

"Who taught you to divide so fairly?" he asked pleasantly.

"I learned a lesson from the Donkey," replied the Fox, carefully edging away.

Learn from the misfortunes of others.

THE DONKEY AND THE LOAD OF SALT

A Merchant, driving his Donkey homeward from the seashore with a heavy load of salt, came to a river crossed by a shallow ford. They had crossed this river many times before without accident, but this time the Donkey slipped and fell when halfway over. And when the Merchant at last got him to his feet, much of the salt had melted away. Delighted to find how much lighter his burden had become, the Donkey finished the journey very gayly.

The next day, the Merchant went for another load of salt. On the way home the Donkey, remembering what had happened at the ford, purposely let himself fall into the water, and again got rid of most of his burden.

The angry Merchant immediately turned about and drove the Donkey back to the seashore, where he loaded him with two great baskets of sponges. At the ford the Donkey again tumbled over; but when he had scrambled to his feet, it was a very disconsolate Donkey that dragged himself homeward under a load ten times heavier than before.

The same measures will not suit all circumstances.

THE NORTH WIND AND THE SUN

THE NORTH WIND and the Sun had a quarrel about which of them was the stronger. While they were disputing with much heat and bluster, a Traveler passed along the road wrapped in a cloak.

"Let us agree," said the Sun, "that he is the stronger who can strip that Traveler of his cloak."

"Very well," growled the North Wind, and at once sent a cold, howling blast against the Traveler.

With the first gust of wind the ends of the cloak whipped about the Traveler's body. But he immediately wrapped it closely around him, and the harder the Wind blew, the tighter he held it to him. The North Wind tore angrily at the cloak, but all his efforts were in vain.

Then the Sun began to shine. At first his beams were gentle, and in the pleasant warmth after the bitter cold of the North Wind, the Traveler unfastened his cloak and let it hang loosely from his shoulders. The Sun's rays grew warmer and warmer. The man took off his cap and mopped his brow. At last he became so heated that he pulled off his cloak, and, to escape the blazing sunshine, threw himself down in the welcome shade of a tree by the roadside.

Gentleness and kind persuasion win where force and bluster fail.

THE HARE AND HIS EARS

THE LION HAD been badly hurt by the horns of a Goat, which he was eating. He was very angry to think that any animal that he chose for a meal, should be so brazen as to wear such dangerous things as horns to scratch him while he ate. So he commanded that all animals with horns should leave his domains within twenty-four hours.

The command struck terror among the beasts. All those who were so unfortunate as to have horns, began to pack up and move out. Even the little Hare, who, as you know, has no horns and so had nothing to fear, passed a very restless night, dreaming awful dreams about the fearful Lion.

And when he came out of the warren in the early morning sunshine, and there saw the shadow cast by his long and pointed ears, a terrible fright seized him.

"Goodbye, neighbor Cricket," he called. "I'm off. He will certainly make out that my ears are horns, no matter what I say."

Do not give your enemies the slightest reason to attack your reputation.

Your enemies will seize any excuse to attack you.

THE WOLF AND THE CRANE

A WOLF HAD been feasting too greedily, and a bone had stuck crosswise in his throat. He could get it neither up nor down, and of course he could not eat a thing. Naturally that was an awful state of affairs for a greedy Wolf.

So away he hurried to the Crane. He was sure that she, with her long neck and bill, would easily be able to reach the bone and pull it out.

"I will reward you very handsomely," said the Wolf, "if you pull that bone out for me."

The Crane, as you can imagine, was very uneasy about putting her head in a Wolf's throat. But she was grasping in nature, so she did what the Wolf asked her to do.

When the Wolf felt that the bone was gone, he started to walk away.

"But what about my reward!" called the Crane anxiously.

"What!" snarled the Wolf, whirling around. "Haven't you got it? Isn't it enough that I let you take your head out of my mouth without snapping it off?"

Expect no reward for serving the wicked.

THE DONKEY IN THE LION'S SKIN

A DONKEY FOUND a Lion's skin left in the forest by a hunter. He dressed himself in it, and amused himself by hiding in a thicket and rushing out suddenly at the animals who passed that way. All took to their heels the moment they saw him.

The Donkey was so pleased to see the animals running away from him, just as if he were King Lion himself, that he could not keep from expressing his delight by a loud, harsh bray. A Fox, who ran with the rest, stopped short as soon as he heard the voice. Approaching the Donkey, he said with a laugh:

"If you had kept your mouth shut you might have frightened me, too. But you gave yourself away with that silly bray."

A fool may deceive by his dress and appearance, but his words will soon show what he really is.

HERCULES AND THE WAGONER

A FARMER WAS driving his wagon along a miry country road after a heavy rain. The horses could hardly drag the load through the deep mud, and at last came to a standstill when one of the wheels sank to the hub in a rut.

The Farmer climbed down from his seat and stood beside the wagon looking at it but without making the least effort to get it out of the rut. All he did was to curse his bad luck and call loudly on Hercules to come to his aid. Then, it is said, Hercules really did appear, saying:

"Put your shoulder to the wheel, man, and urge on your horses. Do you think you can move the wagon by simply looking at it and whining about it? Hercules will not help unless you make some effort to help yourself."

And when the Farmer put his shoulder to the wheel and urged on the horses, the wagon moved very readily, and soon the Farmer was riding along in great content and with a good lesson learned.

Heaven helps those who help themselves.

THE LARK AND HER YOUNG ONES

A Lark made her nest in a field of young wheat. As the stalks grew tall, the young birds, too, grew in strength. Then one day, the Farmer and his son came into the field.

"This wheat is ready for reaping," said the Farmer. "We must call our friends to help us harvest."

This frightened the young Larks, who knew their nest would not be safe from the reapers. They told Mother Lark what they had heard.

"Do not be frightened," said the Mother Lark. "If the Farmer is calling his friends to help, this wheat will not be reaped for a while."

Soon the wheat was so ripe that when the wind shook the stalks, a hail of grains came rustling down on the young Larks' heads.

"If we wait any longer for help," said the Farmer, "we shall lose half the crop. Tomorrow we must set to work ourselves."

When the young Larks told their mother what they had heard that day, she said:

"Then we must leave. When a man decides to do his own work and not depend on anyone else, then you know there will be no more delay." So the next day, when the Farmer and his son cut down the grain, they found an empty nest.

Self-help is the best help.

THE FIGHTING ROOSTERS AND THE EAGLE

ONCE THERE WERE two Roosters living in the same farmyard who could not bear the sight of each other. At last one day they flew up to fight it out, beak and claw. They fought until one of them was beaten and crawled off to a corner to hide.

The Rooster that had won the battle flew to the top of the henhouse, and, proudly flapping his wings, crowed with all his might to tell the world about his victory. But an Eagle, circling overhead, heard the boasting chanticleer and, swooping down, carried him off to his nest.

His rival saw the deed, and coming out of his corner, took his place as master of the farmyard.

Pride goes before a fall.

THE LION AND THE DONKEY

ONE DAY AS the Lion walked proudly down a forest aisle, and the animals respectfully made way for him, a Donkey brayed a scornful remark as he passed.

The Lion felt a flash of anger. But when he turned his head and saw who had spoken, he walked quietly on. He would not honor the fool with even so much as a stroke of his claws.

Do not resent the remarks of a fool. Ignore them.

THE OXEN AND THE WHEELS

A PAIR OF Oxen were drawing a heavily loaded wagon along a miry country road. They had to use all their strength to pull the wagon, but they did not complain.

The Wheels of the wagon were of a different sort. Though the task they had to do was very light compared with that of the Oxen, they creaked and groaned at every turn. The poor Oxen, pulling with all their might to draw the wagon through the deep mud, had their ears filled with the loud complaining of the Wheels. And this, you may well know, made their work so much the harder to endure.

"Silence!" the Oxen cried at last, out of patience. "What have you Wheels to complain about so loudly? We are drawing all the weight, not you, and we are keeping still about it besides."

They complain most who suffer least.

THE FOX AND THE PHEASANTS

One moonlit evening as Master Fox was taking his usual stroll in the woods, he saw a number of Pheasants perched out of his reach on a limb of a tall old tree. The sly Fox soon found a bright patch of moonlight, where the Pheasants could see him clearly; there he raised himself up on his hind legs, and began a wild dance. First he whirled around like a top, then he hopped up and down, cutting all sorts of strange capers. The Pheasants stared giddily. They hardly dared blink for fear of losing him out of their sight a single instant.

Now the Fox made as if to climb a tree, now he fell over and lay still, playing dead, and the next instant he was hopping on all fours, his back in the air, and his bushy tail shaking so that it seemed to throw out silver sparks in the moonlight.

By this time the poor birds' heads were in a whirl. And when the Fox began his performance all over again, so dazed did they become, that they lost their hold on the limb, and fell down one by one to the Fox.

Too much attention to danger may cause us to fall victim to it.

THE DONKEY, THE FOX, AND THE LION

A DONKEY AND a Fox had become close comrades, and were constantly in each other's company. While the Donkey cropped a fresh bit of greens, the Fox would devour a chicken from the neighboring farmyard or a bit of cheese filched from the dairy. One day the pair unexpectedly met a Lion. The Donkey was very much frightened, but the Fox calmed his fears.

"I will talk to him," he said.

So the Fox walked boldly up to the Lion.

"Your Highness," he said in an undertone, so the Donkey could not hear him, "I've got a fine scheme in my head. If you promise not to hurt me, I will lead that foolish creature yonder into a pit where he can't get out, and you can feast at your pleasure."

The Lion agreed and the Fox, grinning at his plan, returned to the Donkey.

"I made him promise not to hurt us," said the Fox. "But come with me, I know a good place that we can hide till he is gone."

So the Fox led the Donkey into a deep pit. But when the Lion saw that the Donkey was his for the taking, he first of all struck down the traitor Fox.

Traitors may expect treachery.

THE DONKEY AND THE GRASSHOPPERS

ONE DAY AS a Donkey was walking in the pasture, he found some Grasshoppers chirping merrily in a grassy corner of the field.

He listened with a great deal of admiration to the song of the Grasshoppers. It was such a joyful song that his pleasure-loving heart was filled with a wish to sing as they did.

"What is it," he asked very respectfully, "that has given you such beautiful voices? Is there any special food you eat, or is it some divine nectar that makes you sing so wonderfully?"

"Yes," said the Grasshoppers, who were very fond of a joke; "it is the dew we drink! Try some and see."

So thereafter the Donkey would eat nothing and drink nothing but dew.

Naturally, the poor foolish Donkey soon died.

The laws of nature are unchangeable.

THE WOLF AND THE LAMB

A STRAY LAMB stood drinking early one morning on the bank of a woodland stream. That very same morning a hungry Wolf came by farther up the stream, hunting for something to eat. As a rule, the Wolf would eat without any reserve, but this Lamb looked so helpless and innocent that the Wolf felt he ought to have an excuse for taking its life.

"How dare you paddle around like that and stir up all the mud!" he shouted. "You deserve to be punished severely!"

"But, Your Highness," replied the Lamb, "I cannot possibly muddy the water you are drinking. You are upstream and I am downstream."

"Well," said the Wolf, "I have heard that you told lies about me last year!"

"How could I have done so?" pleaded the Lamb. "I wasn't born until this year."

"If it wasn't you, it was your brother!"

"I have no brothers."

"Well, then," snarled the Wolf, "it was someone in your family. But regardless, I do not intend to be talked out of my breakfast."

And without another word the Wolf seized the Lamb and carried it off to the forest.

The tyrant can always find an excuse for his tyranny.

The unjust will not listen to the reasoning of the innocent.

THE FARMER AND THE SNAKE

A FARMER WALKED through his field one cold winter morning. On the ground lay a Snake, stiff and frozen with the cold. The Farmer knew how deadly the Snake could be, and yet he picked it up and put it in his bosom to warm it back to life.

The Snake soon revived, and when it had enough strength, bit the man who had been so kind to it. The bite was deadly and the Farmer felt that he must die. As he drew his last breath, he said to those standing around:

Learn from my fate not to take pity on a scoundrel.

THE CAT AND THE BIRDS

A CAT WAS growing very thin. As you have guessed, he did not get enough to eat. One day he heard that some Birds in the neighborhood were ailing and needed a doctor. So he put on a pair of spectacles, and with a leather box in his hand, knocked at the door of the Bird's home.

The Birds peeped out, and Dr. Cat, with much concern, asked how they were. He would be very happy to give them some medicine.

"Tweet, tweet," laughed the Birds. "Very smart, aren't you? We are very well, thank you, and more so, if you only keep away from here."

Be wise and shun the quack.

THE DOG AND HIS MASTER'S DINNER

A Dog had learned to carry his Master's dinner to him every day. He was very faithful to his duty, though the smell of the good things in the basket tempted him.

The Dogs in the neighborhood noticed him carrying the basket and soon discovered what was in it. They made several attempts to steal it from him. But he always guarded it faithfully.

Then one day all the Dogs in the neighborhood got together and met him on his way with the basket. The Dog tried to run away from them. But at last he stopped to argue.

That was his mistake. They soon made him feel so ridiculous that he dropped the basket and seized a large piece of roast meat intended for his Master's dinner.

"Very well," he said, "you divide the rest."

Do not stop to argue with temptation.

THE PLANE TREE

Two Travelers, walking in the noonday sun, sought the shade of a widespreading tree to rest. As they lay looking up among the pleasant leaves, they saw that it was a Plane Tree.

"How useless is the Plane!" said one of them. "It bears no fruit whatever, and only serves to litter the ground with leaves."

"Ungrateful creatures!" said a voice from the Plane Tree. "You lie here in my cooling shade, and yet you say I am useless! Thus ungratefully, O Jupiter, do men receive their blessings!"

Our best blessings are often the least appreciated.

THE FARMER AND THE CRANES

Some Cranes saw a Farmer plowing a large field. When the plowing was done, they watched him sow the seed. It was their feast, they thought.

So, as soon as the Farmer had finished planting, they flew to the field, and began to eat as fast as they could.

The Farmer, of course, knew the Cranes and their ways. He soon returned to the field with a sling. But he did not bring any stones with him. He expected to scare the Cranes just by swinging the sling in the air and shouting loudly at them.

At first the Cranes flew away in fear. But they soon began to see that none of them ever got hurt. They did not even hear the noise of stones flying, and as for words, they would kill nobody. At last they paid no attention whatever to the Farmer.

The Farmer saw that he would have to take other measures to save his grain. So he loaded his sling with stones and killed several of the Cranes. This had the effect the Farmer wanted, for from that day the Cranes visited his field no more.

Bluff and threatening words are of little value with rascals.

Bluff is no proof that hard fists are lacking.

THE MOUSE AND THE WEASEL

A LITTLE HUNGRY Mouse found his way one day into a basket of corn. He had to squeeze himself a good deal to get through the narrow opening between the strips of the basket. But the corn was tempting and the Mouse was determined to get in. When at last he had succeeded, he gorged himself to bursting. Indeed he became about three times as big around the middle as he was when he first went in.

At last he felt satisfied and dragged himself to the opening to get out again. But the best he could do was to get his head out. So there he sat groaning and moaning, both from the discomfort inside him and his anxiety to escape from the basket.

Just then a Weasel came by. He understood the situation quickly.

"My friend," he said, "I know what you've been doing. You've been stuffing yourself with corn. That's what you get. You will have to stay there till you feel just like you did when you went in. Good night, and good enough for you."

And that was all the sympathy the poor Mouse got.

Greediness leads to misfortune.

THE PORCUPINE AND THE SNAKES

A PORCUPINE WAS looking for a good home. At last he found a little sheltered cave, where lived a family of Snakes. He asked them to let him share the cave with them, and the Snakes kindly consented.

The Snakes soon wished they had not given him permission to stay. His sharp quills pricked them at every turn, and at last they politely asked him to leave.

"I am very well satisfied, thank you," said the Porcupine. "I intend to stay right here." And with that, he politely escorted the Snakes out of doors.

Give a finger and lose a hand.

THE WOLVES AND THE SHEEP

A PACK OF Wolves lurked near the Sheep pasture. But the Dogs kept them all at a respectful distance, and the Sheep grazed in safety. So the Wolves devised a plan.

"Why is there such hostility between us?" they said. "If it were not for those Dogs, we should get along beautifully. Send them away and see what good friends we will be."

The Sheep were easily fooled. They persuaded the Dogs to go away, and that very evening the Wolves had the grandest feast of their lives.

Do not give up friends for foes.

THE MAN AND THE LION

A LION AND a Man chanced to travel in company through the forest. They soon began to quarrel, for each of them boasted that he and his kind were far superior to the other both in strength and mind.

Now they reached a clearing in the forest and there stood a statue. It was a representation of Hercules in the act of tearing the jaws of the Nemean Lion.

"See," said the Man, "that's how strong we are! The King of Beasts is like wax in our hands!"

"Ho!" laughed the Lion, "a Man made that statue. It would have been quite a different scene had a Lion made it!"

It all depends on the point of view, and who tells the story.

THE WOLF AND THE SHEPHERD

A WOLF, LURKING near the Shepherd's hut, saw the Shepherd and his family feasting on a roasted lamb.

"Aha!" he muttered. "What a great shouting and running about there would have been, had they caught me at just the very thing they are doing with so much enjoyment!"

Men often condemn others for what they see no wrong in doing themselves.

THE FOX AND THE STORK

ONE DAY, THE Fox thought of a plan to amuse himself at the expense of his friend, the Stork, at whose odd appearance he was always laughing.

"You must come and dine with me today," he said, smiling to himself at the trick he was going to play. The Stork gladly accepted the invitation and arrived in very good appetite.

For dinner the Fox served soup. But it was set out in a very shallow dish, and all the Stork could do was to wet the tip of his bill. Not a drop of soup could he get. But the Fox lapped it up easily, and, to rub it in, made a great show of enjoyment.

The hungry Stork was much displeased at the trick, but he was a calm, even-tempered fellow and he saw no good in flying into a rage. Instead, not long afterward, he invited the Fox to dine with him in turn. The Fox arrived promptly at the time that had been set, and the Stork served a fish dinner that had a very appetizing smell. But it was served in a tall jar with a very narrow neck. The Stork could easily get at the food with his long bill, but all the Fox could do was to lick the outside of the jar, and sniff at the delicious odor. And when the Fox lost his temper, the Stork said calmly:

Do not play tricks on your neighbors unless you can stand the same treatment yourself.